Billie and the Lion

By Evelyn James

Dedicated to my ever supportive family

By Evelyn James

Billie had a lion, she took it into school.

It really scared the teacher but her friends all shouted "COOL!"

It sat down in the classroom and gave a mighty roar.

Teacher looked quite worried, her friends all yelled for MORE!

Then little Suzie Sneddon asked, "What do lions eat"?

Billie shouted "Antelopes, and other types of meat"

They tried to feed him lots of things and lion ate the lot

Like sandwiches and cheesy puffs, and yogurt in a pot

Teacher yelled "Enough of this, please take it to the zoo!"

"Oh don't upset my lion sir, or else he might eat you!"

By now the other teachers had all come out to look

Followed by the janitor, the prefects and the cook

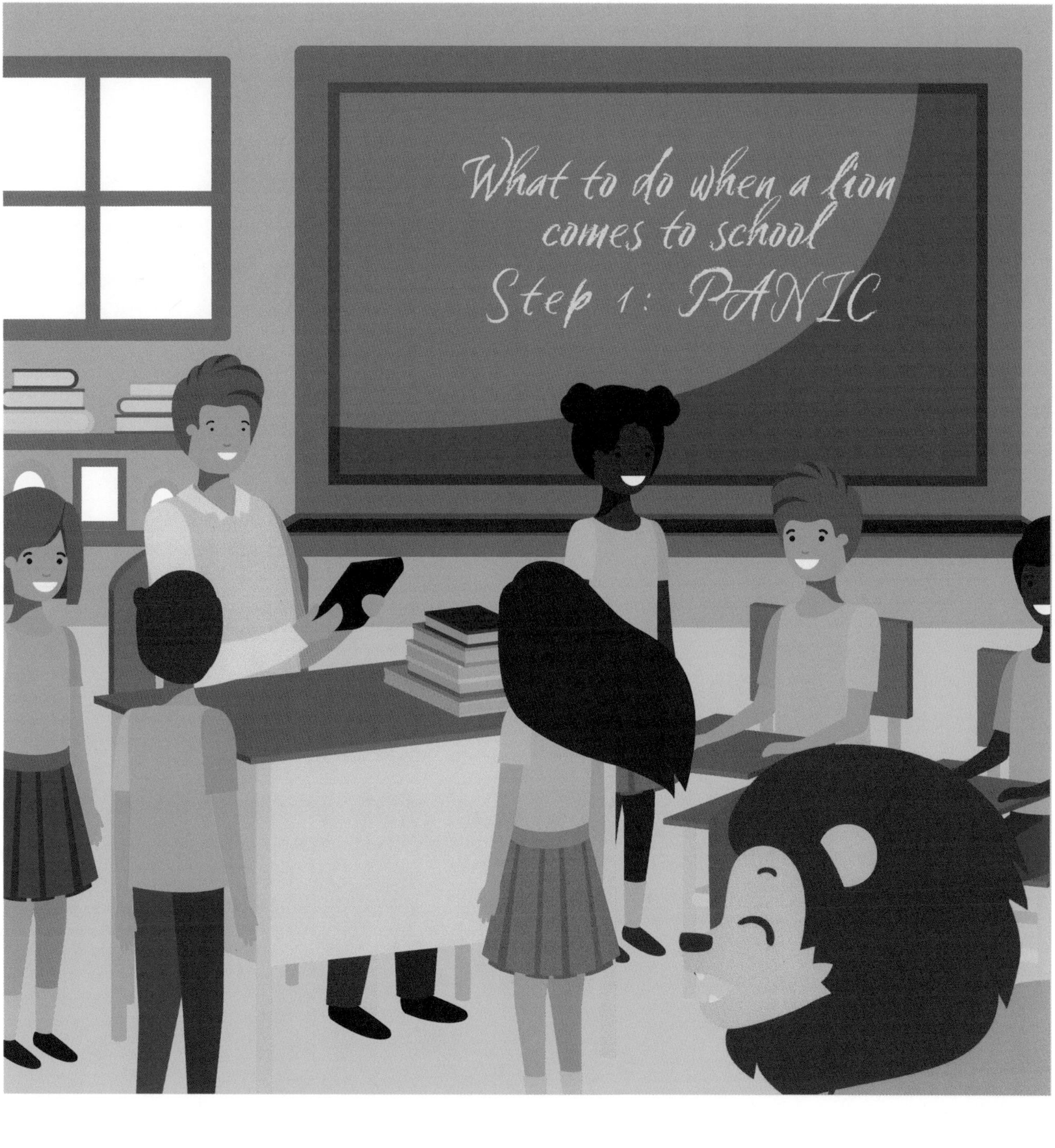
What to do when a lion comes to school
Step 1: PANIC

Someone called the Army, The Navy and the Queen

The local news and TV crews descended on the scene

The whole wide world was watching, as the story grew and grew

On ITV and CNN and even Channel Two

They interviewed a farmer, a policeman and a vet

And anyone who'd ever owned a lion as a pet

The lion simply hung his head and looking very bored

He just curled up and went to sleep, the mighty lion snored.

Billie closed her eyes, for just a second so it seemed

She opened them at home in bed, it had all been a dream

She didn't have a lion, just a fluffy ginger cat

He rolled around and purred at Billie, clawing at the mat

Her mother called out, "Time for school, and don't forget your hat"

Billie left her house for school, but went without the cat

The End

Billie and the Lion

By Evelyn James

Watch out for more
adventures with Billie...

Printed in Great Britain
by Amazon